Duncan
the Dancing Duck

Written and Illustrated by

Syd Hoff

Clarion Books / *New York*

Clarion Books
a Houghton Mifflin Company imprint
215 Park Avenue South, New York, NY 10003
Text and illustrations copyright © 1994 by Syd Hoff

Illustrations executed in ink, watercolor dyes, and colored pencil.
Text is Times Roman.

Library of Congress Cataloging-in-Publication Data

Hoff, Syd, 1912–
    Duncan the dancing duck / by Syd Hoff.
        p.   cm.
    Summary: An irrepressible dancing duck leaves his pond to find fame in the
big city, but after receiving a Golden Duck Award he only wants to return to his family.
    ISBN 0-395-67400-X
        [1. Ducks—Fiction. 2. Dancing—Fiction.]   I. Title.   PZ7.H672Du   1994
[E]—dc20   93-13058

CIP
AC

WOZ 10 9 8 7 6 5 4 3 2 1

For a daughter
who once wanted "quackers" and milk

One day, a little duck started dancing in a pond.

The other little ducks looked at him and laughed.
But their mother didn't think it was funny.

"Please, Duncan," she said,
"stay in line with your brothers and sisters."
But Duncan was having too much fun.

He danced out of the pond

and all around the farm.

The little pigs saw him,
and stayed in the mud with their mother.

The little chickens saw him,
and just kept going about their business.
That didn't stop Duncan!

He went dancing into the farmhouse.
"Well, well, what do we have here?"
asked the farmer.
"It looks like a dancing duck,"
said the farmer's wife.

They watched Duncan dance from room to room
without bumping into furniture.

They watched him dance around the kitchen
without breaking a dish.
"He's good," said the farmer.
"Everybody should see him,"
said the farmer's wife.

They took Duncan to town in their truck.

They took him where there were bright lights
and people going in to see a show.
"Now get out there and do your stuff,"
said the farmer.

Duncan danced on the stage.

He danced in the aisles.
"Hooray for the dancing duck!"
everybody shouted.
"He should have national coverage,"
said the farmer's wife.

They took Duncan to a TV station.

Duncan danced for the cameras.

He appeared on a million sets.

Duncan became so famous,
people chased after him in the street.
They wanted him to sign his name for them.
They wanted one of his feathers.

There were Duncan Fan Clubs everywhere—
even in the Antarctic.

The night of the big show business award,
crowds of fans lined the street in Hollywood.
They cheered as their favorite stars
arrived in limousines.

When Duncan arrived in the truck,
the fans went wild.
"Duncan, Duncan, Duncan!"
they chanted.

The judges gave Duncan a Golden Duck Award.
"Thank you," said Duncan,
and he started dancing.

He danced and he danced until he got so tired,

the farmer and his wife had to carry him.
They took Duncan back to the farm.

Duncan hurried to the pond.
All he wanted now was
to swim, swim, swim with his family.

"Welcome home, Duncan," said his mother.
"You're a good little duck, and I'm proud of you.

"Now please stay in line
with your brothers and sisters."
Duncan was so happy,

he did one more dance
—just for his mother.